P9-DDZ-763

King & King & Family

WITHDRAWN
LVC BISHOP LIBRA

LEBANON VALLEY COLLEGE LIBRARY

Text copyright © 2004 by Linda de Haan & Stern Nijland
Illustrations copyright © 2004 by Linda de Haan & Stern Nijland

All rights reserved. No part of this book may be reproduced in any form without
the written permission of the publisher, except in the case of brief quotations embodied
in critical articles or reviews.

Tricycle Press
a little division of Ten Speed Press
P.O. Box 7123
Berkeley, California 94707
www.tenspeed.com

English adaptation of story by Abigail Samoun
Book design by Betsy Stromberg
Typeset in Stone Hinge
The illustrations in this book were rendered in mixed media.

Library of Congress Cataloging-in-Publication Data

Haan, Linda de, 1965-
  King & King & family / Linda de Haan & Stern Nijland.
    p. cm.
Summary: King Lee and King Bertie take a honeymoon trip to the jungle
and bring home a surprise.
  ISBN 1-58246-113-9
  [1. Kings, queens, rulers, etc.--Fiction. 2. Homosexuality--Fiction. 3.
Adoption--Fiction.] I. Title: King and King and family. II. Nijland,
Stern, 1976- III. Title.
PZ7.H11132 Ki 2004
[E]--dc22

                              2003018261

First printing, 2004
Printed in China

1 2 3 4 5 6 — 08 07 06 05 04

After their royal wedding, King and King took a honeymoon trip to a land far from their kingdom.

"My, this is a very heavy suitcase!"
"You see, there's nothing to worry about."

"Look! It's our friend the Crown Kitty!

"How nice to have you along," said King Lee.

The three
travelers hiked
into the jungle...

where it seemed as if all the animals and their babies had turned out to greet them.

"Such good parents!" said King Lee.

"What a happy little one!"

The mosquitoes had also turned out to greet them.

"They sure do like you, Bertie!"

They crossed a
rope bridge,

soared through
the trees,

passed by papa and
his baby,

and finally reached
the river.

They paddled downstream all afternoon.

"Quick!" said King Lee. "Take a picture of the hippo family!"

As evening fell, it grew quite dark.

They took turns keeping watch.

King Bertie whispered, "Did you see that?"

But King Lee was sleeping soundly.

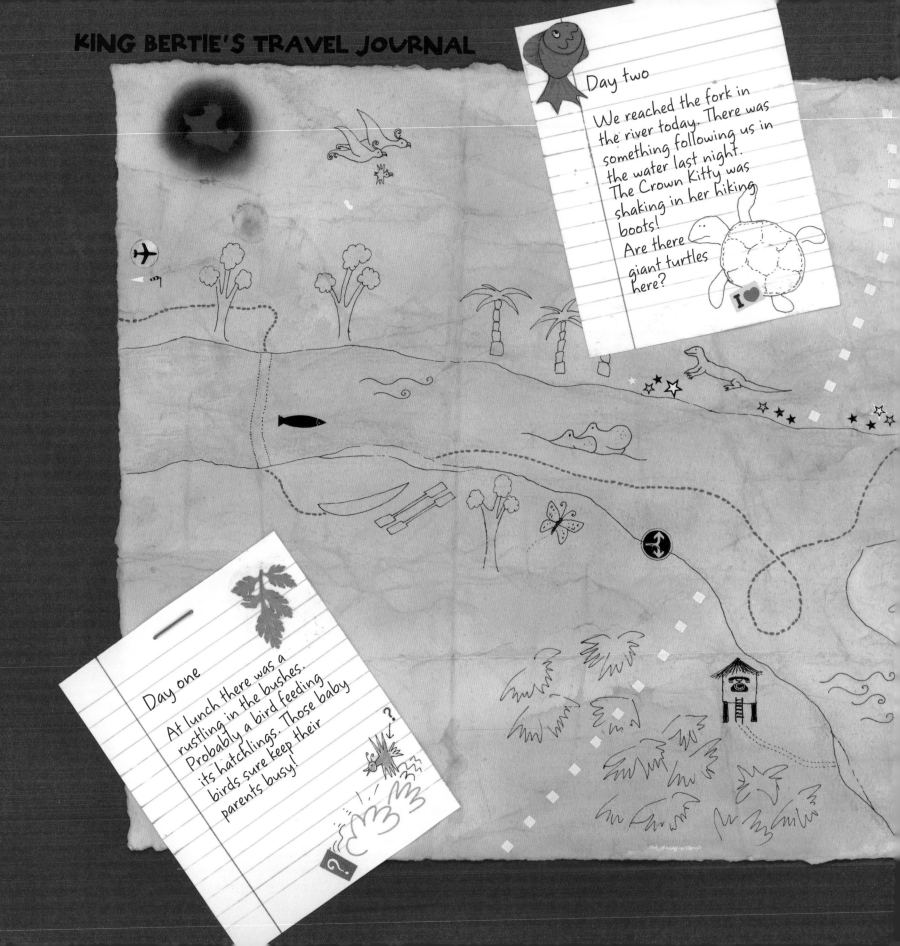

Day two

We reached the fork in the river today. There was something following us in the water last night. The Crown Kitty was shaking in her hiking boots!

Are there giant turtles here?

Day one

At lunch there was a rustling in the bushes. Probably a bird feeding its hatchlings. Those baby birds sure keep their parents busy!

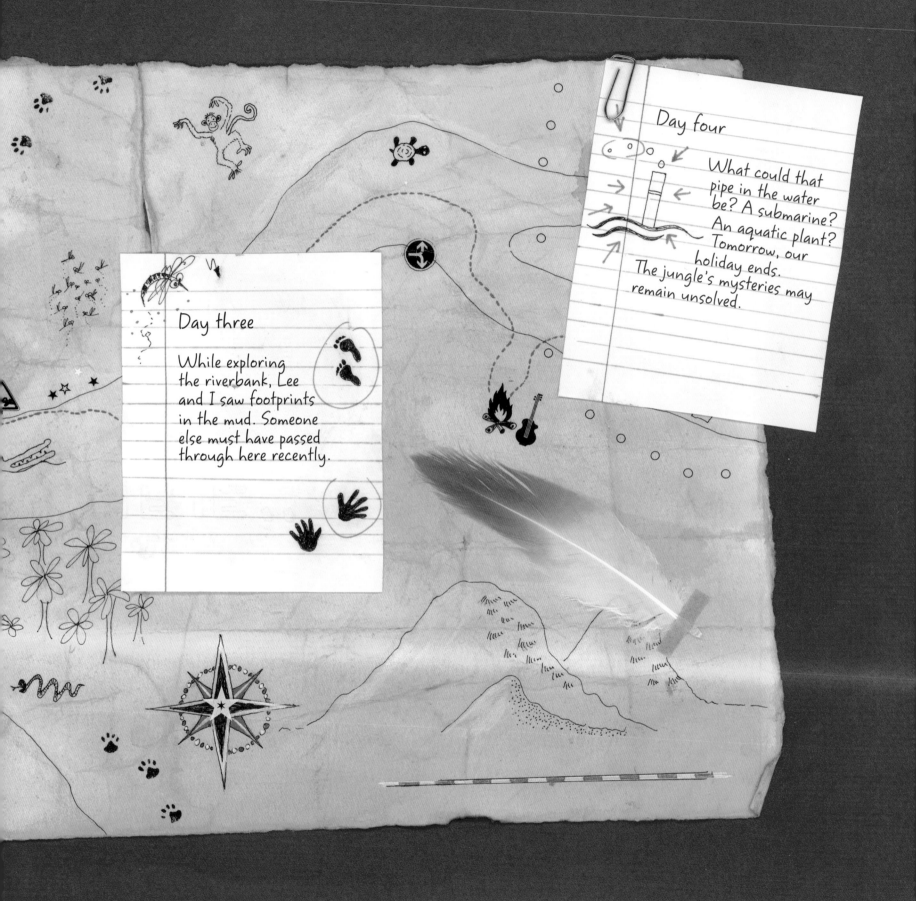

Day three

While exploring the riverbank, Lee and I saw footprints in the mud. Someone else must have passed through here recently.

Day four

What could that pipe in the water be? A submarine? An aquatic plant? Tomorrow, our holiday ends. The jungle's mysteries may remain unsolved.

and they brought with them a very **heavy** suitcase.

All at once, the suitcase **burst** open.

"Oh, MY, it's a little girl from the jungle!" said the Queen.

surprise

"You're the child we've always wanted," said King and King.

She told them all about her adventures.

To make it
official, King and
King adopted
the little girl
who had traveled
so far to be with them.
This took lots of documents
and stamps.

At last the big day has come for Princess Daisy. Her daddies make a big fuss, and everyone has a good time at the party.

What a happy little one!

LEBANON VALLEY COLLEGE LIBRARY